Was It Love?

Vriddhi Dua

Was It Love? By **Vriddhi Dua**

This book is a work of fiction. All the names, characters, events and incidents are either the work of the author's imagination or derived from certain life instances experienced by the author herself. Any resemblance to the same, in living or dead, is a mere coincidence.

This book is sold subject to the condition that it shall not, by any way of trade or otherwise, be lent, resold or hired out, circulated and no reproduction in any form, in whole or part (except for brief quotations in critical articles or reviews) may be made without the permission of the author.

This book has been published in good faith that the work of the author is original. All efforts have been taken to make the material error-free. However, the author and the publisher disclaim the responsibility for any inadvertent errors.

Genre: Fiction, Romance

Acknowledgement

Thank You, dear reader and friend, for picking up **Was it Love?**

As I write this, a sense of excitement mixed with nervousness topped with a lot of other emotions is racing up and down my spine. But let's just pretend normal (as we do every day) and appreciate this moment.

This brainchild is very close to my heart not because it is my debut novel but also for the many learnings it has given me as a writer and as a person. The fact that it has some prominent instances taken out from the depth of some of my most ridden closets makes me very emotional. I'd like to, hence, extend my sincerest gratitude to the very moments and experiences of life that made me pen them down into this beautiful masterpiece.

Thanks to my amazing designer friend, Urvashi Sharma, for bringing out the best in the book cover.

Next, I'd like to extend my heartiest gratitude to my family and the centre of my universe - my Mom, Mrs Anjali without whom I wouldn't have been who I am today. She deserves nothing but the best in life!

Thank you to you and all the ever-amazing readers for giving me a chance to touch your lives through this book. Thank you for reading this book which holds a special place in my life. You guys are truly awesome! Thank you to my lovely Instagram family which is growing only stronger and bigger, for accepting me and motivating me to do better! You guys not only deserve but duly command my love.

Thank you to the higher calling who never makes me lose hope and navigates me to pursue my dreams. Thank you to the universe for giving me the wonderful life I have and the unknown which is coming!

Through this book and other mediums of entertainment including YouTube, Social Platforms and others, I want to reach out to as many people as possible. Being a human, I know I can falter and I shall have my ups and downs. If possible, do support me through the process and help in keeping the good in me going!

Lastly, I thank you from the bottom of my heart for having me enter your life. And as much as you admire someone, I would request you to only love me. Because as Chethan Bhagat says, 'Admiration passes,

Love endures. Admiration comes with expectations, but love accepts flaws.'

Thank You! Thank You! Thank You!

Welcome to the family! Happy Reading!

Yours lovingly
Vriddhi

"Love is an untamed force. When we try to control it, it destroys us. When we try to imprison it, it enslaves us. When we try to understand it, it leaves us feeling lost and confused."

— Paulo Coelho

Prologue

'So, are we calling it quits', He conceded.

I looked at him in the eye, and squirmed, 'Is that even a question now?'

Those deep, dark eyes which once had my heart swirl were now filled with empty hopes and nothingness. I couldn't recognize him anymore. There we were, like two strangers having that awkward phase of trying to crack a sane conversation on a sofa, facing each other.

'You make it sound as if it was all my fault. Aren't you equally to be blamed? Let me remind you, it is you who is moving out of this relationship, not me.', he claimed.

I felt disgusted. I gathered my emotions,

gulped down a breath, and with sheer disappointment released what had been hidden in the corners of my heart since forever, 'I never said you are the only one at fault, Abir. But have you given me any reason to stay in this relationship? I just can't do this to me anymore… This relationship was never ours Abir, it was just yours, I was just a tool for you to ride on for your expenses, your guilt, your emotional imbalance, your physical needs, your everything. Where was I? Where were us?'

Tears rolled down my eyes and that feeling of a knife piercing through my heart, deeper and deeper surpassed all emotions. I was numb.

'You don't have to do this Kalpana,' he deflected. 'I know I've been an asshole throughout, but that doesn't mean we'll end this. We were so…' he stopped mid-sentence.

'We were so different. We have always been so different,' I yakked. 'Relationships are meant to mend two hearts, it is about passing through the odds and evens of time, hand in hand and improving each other, making each other better! It is not about one ruling over the other, it is not about shouting your gut out on someone at your will, it is not about forcing the other to fulfil your needs, it is not about telling the other one that you aren't good enough, it is not what we had between the two of us, Abir,' I screamed.

He looked around and gave me that 'Oh damn' look for the millionth time, straightened his pose and spoke, 'As you say. You want to leave, you can. I'll pay for whatever spends you have made on me - for my phone, the dates we had, the clothes I wear, everything. Let me know the amount. I might not be able to pay back instantly, maybe in chunks. But I will pay. Can I leave now? I have my friends waiting for me to go down for *chai sutta*.' He sulked at the thought of returning the money.

'Are we having a deal out here? Can you give me back the moments I had spent with you? Can you erase the painful memories you've given me? Can you take back your insulting words you've used for me time and again?' I wailed.

It was our tea break in the office. And since none in the office were aware of our so-called relationship, none knew he was with me. 'Chai sutta' is a thing we used to say every time we had to go down to have tea (chai) and a cigarette (sutta).

I took a deep breath and pursed my lips. I

was left aghast.

He looked at me, scratched his head and left the room.

There I was, terribly hurt by the man I had loved with all my heart and soul sobbing, all by self. There was nothing left to say. I had given way too much to make this work and he had received way more than he needed, I guess. I sobbed until I couldn't breathe, I just couldn't believe we were 'us' no more. And all I was left with were regrets, deep hurt and an aching heart. I stood to walk out of that room where a part of my life had a brutal end. But before I could take a step forward, I felt weak in the knees and fell flat on the surface. The world was taking rounds faster than the Earth moved around the orbit, I could sense blood oozing out the corner of my forehead and heart sinking with just one question I muttered - *'Was it love?'*

... And everything came to a standstill.

Chapter 1 | New Beginnings

'Yayyyyy!! We're finally done with it!' shouted a bunch of girls while moving out of the examination hall.

My boards just got over! And I couldn't be more excited! A sense of relief went through my nerves and I could feel the load off my shoulders finally. Finally, I could sleep as much as I wanted, eat to my heart's content, binge watch my favourite web series and party with my friends. It was indeed the freedom we all were craving for.

As I was walking down the lane, I heard someone calling my name.

'Is he...' I mumbled and turned around with excitement. It was him!

'Heyy! You left your book at the bench, so thought of returning!' He exclaimed.

I had goosebumps. He was my first and only crush in school and I couldn't believe he was talking to me. Lucky girl, I thought to myself.

'I…. I… I think I missed it by mistake,' I had to literally pinch myself to stop fumbling.

He smiled.

Kiyaan belonged to the 'popular gang' of our batch. And although most of the members of that group were all fancy and show off, Kiyaan was a sweetheart. We were bench-mates for 3 weeks and 4 days (Yes, I was helluva crazy for him!). We had eye contacts, awkward moments, exchanged shy smiles and sometimes helped each other in the weekly tests. Life was amazing until one of his group girls took him away from me in the name of friendship and he couldn't refuse. And since then, all we shared were distance-glances each time either of us crossed our paths.

'So... I'd take a leave I guess, we're going to some club to party..' he said.

After staring back at him for exactly 15 seconds, I said, 'Umm yeah. We're going to Select City Walk I think too.'

Please don't leave - I was sending messages to him through my brain as if I were some sort of a hypnotic.

After about a minute of waiting for each other to make a move, he finally waved and walked away...slowly.

I smiled wryly, knowing I might never get a

chance to see him again. Or maybe I could if God will be kind. We left anyway.

***

25 days had passed since our boards happened. Life suddenly became all boring and sad. Seeing my mom suffer from a deadly disease each day at home was tough. It was tough to see her survive on medicines and undergo painful treatments every week.

I had to do something.

'Mom, I am planning to drop my regular college degree to get a job. I think I can manage a graduate degree alongside. What do you think?' I asked her while she was chopping onions.

She looked at me. I couldn't decide whether it was the anger or helplessness, but she screamed at me at the top of her voice,

'What do I think? If you've made up your mind, do as you please. Who listens to me in this house anyway?'

Typical Indian Mom, my brain cells squirmed at me.

I shared, 'It's not like that Ma... You know our family condition. No one is earning, we barely are able to meet our expenses with the savings we have. You are already spending a dime on Karan. And until he doesn't start earning, we'll have to manage. I can't be so selfish.' I had to be honest here.

Karan, my elder brother, was pursuing engineering from a private college. Mom's eyes filled with tears. I know if I asked her, she would just blame it on the onions. Some things are better to be left unsaid.

She straightened her face and with all her

poise said, 'It is your life, you need to decide. Whatever decision you make today will affect your whole life. Make a wise one.'

And she left for the kitchen.

That night, I couldn't sleep. I loved the college vibe and had been dreaming of living the hostel life, partying with friends, gossiping of crushes and trips and so much more. As the fan on the ceiling was taking rounds, so were my thoughts.

It was not until the next morning that I made the decision.

***

I had decided to take up a job and manage my graduation by myself. I knew this would affect my life drastically, but I had to choose the 'Road not taken'. I still remembered that poem by Robert Frost, it surely had an impact on me.

One of my friends was joining a BPO to spend the month-long vacation to earn and possibly learn something - communication skills were important, you see. And as a good friend, he had referred me for the job too. So, today's my interview.

I had partially convinced my mom to let me go do this job for a month and then see what we do. I had also promised her to fill forms for competitive exams and try to get into a good college. Only for the namesake, I knew it inside.

Since it was my very first interview and I didn't really have any confidence or skills to crack it, I was quite sure I'm going to commit some mistake or the other, like always! But to my surprise, I got through.

'Is it God's signal?' I asked myself as the interviewer was prepping for the final rounds of the payout discussion.

'Any questions?' The interviewer asked. I said no, not really.

'Fine,' she exclaimed. Adding further, 'At the moment, we can pay you 10k a month plus incentives for the sales you hit according to our incentive slab. After a few months, if we see your performance improve, we might give you a raise but that totally depends on how you perform.'

I didn't know whether to say yes or no. Whether it was a good package or not. I was just out of the house to earn something. And this seemed certainly better than the blurred figures I had in mind.

'Oh wait,' she scanned through my documents and stared at me, straight in the eye.

'You're not yet 18. We can't hire you,' she deciphered.

'Well, It's my last day of being 17. Tomorrow is my birthday,' I justified.

'Bravo, you can join with the next batch on 23rd May. Welcome aboard,' she said while gathering her files and rushed out of the room.

Chapter 2 | Love At First Sight

23.05.2014

'Oh! I'm sorry.' I whispered while bending down to pick up a few files. Bumping straight into a guy on the very first day of my job was quite a good job, indeed.

Okay, awkward moment.

Eyes locked. None of us took our eyes off each other. There he was, a tall, wheatish guy with a semi-muscular build staring into my eyes. I think the glare went for a good 30 seconds until I realized he was speaking to me.

'It's… alright. New joinee?' He questioned.

I straightened the end of my kurta,

shrugged away the dirt and said, 'Yes. First-day nervousness I guess. Sorry about that.'

'Oh, no worries. Chill! You'd do just fine. 3 days in training and a few mock calls and you'd be rocking it. Trust me!' He smiled.

I think he noticed me fidgeting my fingers and was just trying to make it all cool for me. But it felt so good to hear him say those soothing words to me.

'By the way Hi, I'm Abir.' He introduced himself while extending his hand.

'Kalpana.' I smiled while responding to the gesture. His skin felt warm and comforting.

'See you soon.' He winked and turned away to move in the direction of his cabin.

Was I blushing? I asked myself. I had developed the hots for Abir. I turned away anyway to find my way to the training room and waited patiently.

***

'It's pretty hot out here, could you please turn on the AC?' someone asked the peon who came to serve us coffee.

I spent the next one hour noticing what my fellow batchmates were doing and judging them by their weird expressions. It was quite hilarious. Looking at their faces, I had figured out that all of us belonged to the age group of 18-25.

The guy sitting at the opposite corner was checking out girls walking outside our cabin (courtesy: the glass door), two girls were busy doing (rather, overdoing) their makeup, another guy was having mental calculations of some kind while the one sitting right next to him was poking his nose.

Good start of the day, LOL, I told myself.

We waited for another 45 minutes until the HR came in along with my friend to make an announcement.

'Sorry guys, the trainer was occupied with some important tasks. He'd be here in an hour. Till then, you can have your lunch and see around the office. Good luck!' She said and left.

My friend came in to call me for lunch. He was the only face I was familiar with among the dozens around. We had a good time during lunch and he showed me our office post which we headed for a quick walk outside.

***

It took me nearly 15 minutes to head back to the training room which meant I'd be 10 minutes late. First day and two goof-ups already. I could see where I was heading already.

I saw the trainer writing something on the board and felt as though I had seen him somewhere but couldn't figure out where. I knocked on the door and slipped inside silently to not disturb the session.

The trainer turned around to see who's late and oh my god, to my delight it was him. Abir. He smiled slyly and turned back to the board to continue with the session.

The session went well and Abir made sure to make us comfortable in the new environment.

We stayed in the cabin till 5 PM and were given an early release that day. Two more days of training were left before we would be handed over the mikes and systems. I was already excited to get to the job and start working.

***

It was noon on the third day of our training and a Saturday.

Abir was still in the cabin training us while my friend waited patiently outside the cabin for the session to get over.

After nearly 15 minutes, Abir released us. While other trainees were moving out of the room, I waited patiently to get to talk to Abir. I knew it was the last day to be around him and I wanted to make the most of it.

As I stood up and walked towards the door, he spoke, 'Boyfriend?'

'No no! We're just friends. We live colonies apart!' I responded.

Wait. Did he just check if I have a boyfriend? Does this mean something? Should I ask if he has a girlfriend? Or should I take it slow? Gosh, I was already going mad.

The lunch was pretty much the usual. We ate in my friend's team bay, had fun checking out other people, went for a walk and came back just in time. I couldn't afford to make a third mistake I knew. The following hours had some extensive training and a mock call session for us.

I was least interested in the theory of why we do what we do and how we do what we are supposed to do. My eyes couldn't move away from his eyes. Oh, man! Those deep, dark eyes carrying a sea of emotions and secrets inside them. If only we could have some more room for just the two of us minus the remaining crowd, it would have been perfect.

During the mock call session, everyone was asked to go on the system and attend a call by Abir where he would pretend to be the prospect and we would have to handle his queries.

I watched Abir take rounds of my fellow batchmates. His hands moving to and fro smoothly while talking, his eyes positioned at the wall in front of him, his legs spread out wide and loose and his back relaxing against the cushion of the chair.

Finally, my turn came. I sat on the hot seat,

put on my headphones and clicked the button on the screen to call Abir. I was equally excited and nervous.

Abir picked up the phone and took two deep breaths. I got goosebumps. I felt a sudden rush through my body, butterflies in my stomach and heartbeat running faster than Usain Bolt running on a racetrack. It was magical.

He spelt out his first sentence, 'Hello there. I had a query for the latest product.'

His voice was deeper than the deep blue sea with a sense of calmness and comfort, slightly hoarse with a soft rhythm and extremely soothing. I was already in love.

The call went fine. Better than I expected and worse than what he would have expected from me. But it was good for a novice like me. We cheered for each other after our last session and bid each other goodbyes before we would start our jobs officially the coming Monday.

I went back home with a weird feeling. I was excited about the job to start because the training days were quite boring but I wasn't very happy. After all, Abir would not be around for the rest of my job. Those three days were manageable only because of him. Within 3 days, he had captured my mind in full capacity. There was nothing else I could think of and nothing else I would want to think of except him. I didn't feel this way for anyone before. Hormones maybe? Or the age? Or pure mad love? I couldn't decide who to blame.

Chapter 3 | 6 Months Later

'Good job, you cracked it hell again!' cheered my Team Lead. I smiled back wryly. All of us knew why he was so happy, our performances had a big impact on his incentives after all!

The weather had changed and it was surprisingly too cold inside the office. I was in my usual kurta and leggings with no jackets or shawl to cover myself. I had spent most of the day sipping hot cups of coffee and tea while attending customer calls. By now I had realised most of HR's promises are fake and I am not going to get the much-awaited appraisal anytime soon. But since I had no time to spend the money, I had spent most of it except for the usual travel expenses and small parties we used to conduct in our team sometimes. My friend had also left by now to join Concentrics, leaving me with a bunch of crazy individuals with no such identity of their own. Life had suddenly become so mundane.

In these months, I barely got a chance to interact with Abir. He used to rush back from work as soon as the clock struck 6:30 and would enter just in time to make sure he wasn't late. Majority of my friends and colleagues gossiped about the 'stud' in our office. Exactly, Abir. He was even linked with a couple of girls who were decent looking. I would hush away the rumours and wonder why everyone's after him. Jealous maybe?

Oh, and I was also convinced that nothing could ever happen between me and Abir. Because I didn't look like any of the girls he was linked with, wasn't the prettiest, didn't touch makeup at all and wasn't skinny either. I was healthy and would struggle to hide my bulges at times under extra-sized kurtas and black had become my all-time saviour.

It was 4:00 in the evening and I couldn't deal with the cold anymore. I started looking around in search of a spare cloth I could cover myself with after asking for it, obviously. I wouldn't snap at anyone for not lending me their belongings any way!

Finally, I got sight of a sleeveless jacket wrapped on a chair. I rushed to that team and looked around to find the owner of the jacket I was desperately wanting to wear.

'Excuse me, whose jacket is this?' I asked, cross-armed and shivering.

'Mine.' I heard someone call.

I turned around and there he was. Abir.

'You're feeling cold, is it?' He responded, glaring at me.

'Umm… yes actually. Could you lend me your jacket for some time if you aren't using it?' I replied.

'All yours!' He replied back with his quirky smile.

'Thanks.' I took hold of the jacket and walked away, slowly. I didn't want to though, of course. We were facing each other after 6 long months! 6 LONG MONTHS.

***

6:00 PM, The Same Day

'Abir has been looking out for you for quite some time, you seem to be his next target,' Arpita said and winked at me.

We were the two best friends in the office everyone knew of. We would have lunch together, hang out during tea breaks and share all the gossip in the office with each other.

'Shut up, will you!' I appealed. My cheeks went rent and butterflies were taking rounds in my stomach already.

Getting out of the dream zone, I quickly stood up, removed his jacket which I had been wearing for more than an hour and went in search of him.

'Hey, there you go.' I smirked with his jacket in my hand, facing his back.

He turned towards me and said, 'I have been looking for...'

Before he could finish his sentence, I took

his hand and kept the jacket on it. 'Thank me later,' I chirped.

'Haha! Well, it seems someone is having good fun in this office.'

'Because someone trained me well for the job.' I winked.

'You know what, give me your number. It'll be easier for me to track you then.' He said with a short laugh.

'995-------' I responded faster than the bullet train moved on its track, my oxytocin and dopamine being fully charged up in an instant.

'Good, let's be in touch. See you Kalpana.'

I heard him say my name after so long. This is definitely more than special, I thought to myself.

***

As soon as I reached home, I changed and served myself dinner. Mom wasn't talking to me properly since we had a tiff over me joining a regular college vs correspondence. And I had to choose the latter, we weren't financially secure. I had to step up before things went further down the drain.

Abir hadn't texted me yet. I ate my dinner and surfed the internet for a bit and was ready to doze off until I heard the bubble sound on my phone. Message received.

'Hey! It's me, Abir. What's up?'

'Hi, quite early, I'm impressed.' I replied.

'Sorry, boys you know! We went off for drinks... Just returned home.' He responded.

'Well, someone is quite busy.'

'Not as much as you little princess.'

Did he just call me princess? Isn't he the sweetest? This was the very first time I had been actually enjoying a conversation with a man. All of my online dates had been pretty awful and the ones I wanted to be serious with, demanded something else.

'Hello? Slept already?' He texted again.

'Uh, not at all! I was just prepping for the morning breakfast. Gotta cook in the morning!' I answered.

'Ooh, La La! Miss multi-talented.' He remarked.

'Certainly lesser than Mr Busy *winks' I bellowed.

We chatted for over 2 hours until we went off to sleep. Yes, we slept together, in our own beds, at the same time. I was right, this is special, I smiled at my silly thoughts as I shut my eyes to enter the dreamland.

Chapter 4 | Snarls and Squiddles

Within a span of 2 months, we had become very close. The funny part, however, was that we would never make our friendship public. He didn't want to be linked again or be tagged as a casanova again. But I was still happy about our little something.

'You're becoming the highlight of the office girl! What's cooking, tell me?!' Arpita smirked.

'LOL! You're just overreacting. *Aisa kuch nahi hai!*' I begged.

Let me be honest with you here, whenever someone says - '*Aisa kuch nahi hai*' (It's nothing like that), know that something is fishy. So yes, I was obviously pretending to be totally unaware of what Arpita was saying.

'Dude! Do you know that Abir is being linked with you these days? I too feel something is cooking between you and him. I don't like him. Tell me it's a lie!' Arpita said in one breath.

I turned away and replied, 'No… It's nothing like that ya! We do talk about work sometimes, but nothing more than that. Relax!'

Arpita took a breath of relief. This was the only secret I had hidden from her under the deepest of my closets. And I had to keep it buried until it turns out to be something potential.

We headed for lunch. I ate silently, to avoid any such questions. I was really bad at lying and this hiding thing was already getting on my nerves.

We had just set out for a walk right after lunch as usual when I heard my phone's bell ring.

It was Mr Busy.

For obvious reasons, I had not added his real name. Quite like our teenage days, when we would name our boyfriends as girlfriends in our phones and vice versa. And hello? I was still a teen, so don't judge!

'Hey!' I blushed.

'Hey, Kalpana. I'm stuck up. I need your help ya.' Abir responded, tensed.

'Tell me? What happened?'

'I need some money. I've lost a bet to someone and need to pay back right now to him. You know these guys ya, I'd be doomed if I don't pay them.' He begged.

'How much do you need?' I responded instantaneously. He had asked me, out of everybody else for help and I couldn't refuse.

'5000 bucks. I'm waiting for you near the ATM. Reach ASAP!'

Seems he had planned already. Without thinking for even a second, I rushed inside the office, took out my card and headed straight to meet Abir near the ATM. Me, who had been working for a reason, earning for a bigger reason, kept everything aside and ran to him - who I wasn't sure would ever be mine.

I gave him the cash anyway. He didn't tell

me he had taken a short leave that day. Neither did he tell me of any plans that he had set up right after taking the money.

I spent the whole evening waiting for his call like he did on other days, stayed awake till 3 in the night to receive a message. But he neither called or texted.

A galore of doubts clouded my mind. Was I overdoing things? Should I pretend to say no first and let him nag a bit? Does he know that I have feelings for him? What if what others say turns out to be right? What if we remain friends forever? What if.

***

14.02.2015

Days passed. And then a month, then another. Things went back to normal. Abir hadn't paid back yet but we would talk every day like we had started. Although, he would remind me now and then that he would pay back soon. I just wasn't sure when.

'Happy Valentine's Day my love' chirped Arpita.

'Would have sounded good if you were a boy, silly!' I laughed. We giggled and got back to our work. My eyes, still searching for him.

Throughout the day, my mind and heart were battling for the most important question of the day - should I go and wish him? Or should I wait and let him wish me first? Aah! Crazy Love, I tell you!

I couldn't get a chance to see or hear from Abir the whole day which made me really upset until I was punching out to leave the office and there I saw him.

'Hey! Someone is in a rush, I see!' he joked.

'Naah! Someone seems to be lost today.' I sighed with a sad face and started to walk down the stairs until I heard him say…

'Happy Valentine's Day Kalpana!' He wished, smiling.

I looked up and responded, 'Oh! Was it today?' pretending as if I didn't know.

'Yes, little princess!'

'Thanks! Happy Valentine's Day to you too… Mr Busy!'

And I left for home. With a not-so-good mood, I entered my house and rushed straight to my room. I threw my bag on my bed and fell flat on it, a drop of tear rolled down my eye. Did it hurt?

I made my preps for my class the next day. Correspondence batches had their classes on Sundays in the same buildings where regular batches would study, we just got the whole week's dose of studies in one day. Everything was slow and sad until I received a text… and it was him again!

'Hey! What are you doing tomorrow?' Abir questioned.

'Nothing, Would go and attend my classes. North campus is quite far though :(' I answered.

'Well then! I have a better plan! Let's go to CP, what say?'

I read that message five times before I could gain my senses. Did he just ask me out? My innermost voices shouted with glee.

'What time?'

'12:00 PM at the Rajiv Chowk metro station.'

'Done.'

'Good girl! See you tomorrow.'

'Night.'

'Night Night. :)'

Chapter 5 | First Date

15.02.2015

Mom knew I had college so I didn't have to convince anyone to let me go out on a Sunday which would otherwise have been warfare. That meant I could get ready and leave on time without being questioned. What a lovely start!

For a change, I wore a suit, filled my eyes with kajal and applied multiple layers of my lip balm with a pinkish tinge on my lips to act like the sexy ladies getting ready for their dinner dates. The only mismatch was the figure and the amount of makeup they applied to look good.

I reached CP by 12:15 PM and the weather was scorching hot. I was looking around to find him. Man, I was so waiting for this day (oops, date!) to happen!!

'What are you looking for when your date is here?' He said.

Did he just say date? OH MY GOD!!

'Trying to find the reason why the busiest guy is acting so sweet today, mind telling me?' I played along.

'Because it's time for us to head to Bangla Sahib and seek some blessings. Let's go' He was too good with his answers.

We went inside the gurdwara, he covered his head with a scarf available at the entrance while I veiled my head. We walked side by side and sat near Sarovar Maharaj (a holy pond) quietly. Sitting there in silence was so peaceful. My heart squiddled with joy. It was the best moment frozen in time.

Seeing us sitting beside each other, an old uncle from a corner came rushing towards us with a stick and in his old, grumpy tone, shouted, 'Newly married huh? Go sit and pray inside. You are not allowed to sit here.'

Abir and I looked at each other and giggled. We stood up and started walking towards the main hall. As luck would have it, I mistakenly stepped on the surface barefoot, jumped with a squeak, stepped on boiling water (courtesy the sun) and slipped.

Abir came rushing to get hold of me. I was extremely embarrassed.

We did our prayers, ate at McDonald's and went to sit in Central Park, facing each other.

'Wait, there is something on your... Did you

apply lipstick today? Special, hmmm!' He teased.

I blushed.

Changing the topic, he asked, 'It's a good date. Isn't it?'

'Is it a date?' I smirked.

Before he could say something, his phone rang and he went awkward. He looked at the screen of his phone, put it on silent, kept it back in the pocket of his jeans and looked away.

'Kalpana, I want to tell you something. I don't know how you would react but I think now it's time.'

'Is everything alright?' I asked, tensed.

'I don't know how to start. I'm sorry about

what I'm going to tell you. But I have to.'

'Shoot.' I replied, eager to hear his story.

'You remember the day I asked you for money? It wasn't for any money. I... I... I had to celebrate my girlfriend's birthday. I had no money left with me and she wanted to go to places and have a good one and I couldn't resist. I will...' He shared.

'Pay me back? I hope someday. You could have said the truth and taken the money, I wouldn't say no. But anyway, go ahead, I'm listening.'

'Well, I know. But I didn't want you to feel bad. I met Nisha in our office. She was here for just a month before you joined. We dated for quite long but then I found out that she was cheating on me. And very slyly, broke up and went away. But I loved her for real. I know people call me the stud in the office and casanova and what not. But I loved her. So when she wanted to come back, I couldn't refuse. She was suffering from Tuberculosis. She needed my care and attention.'

He took a few deep breaths and continued, 'The reason I asked you to call me and wake me up every day was that I could wake up early and cook meals for her. I would do it every single day and wait for her at our common bus stop, stay on the bus for however long she is and then come to the office. The reason why I left on time was that I had to reach the bus stop before her so that I get to spend some more time with her.'

I was shocked. I bought a bottle of water from a local seller walking around us and emptied half the bottle in one sip. He noticed my act and waited patiently for me to be ears again.

'But over time, I realised this isn't working out. She has used me too much for too long. And with you, it is something special. You care for me, you understand me and I know you…' He stopped mid-sentence.

He looked at me in the eye and said, 'Look Kalpana, I'm sorry. I know I've been really selfish all these days but I am willing to get out of this. And only you can help me.'

His pleads sounded genuine and after a few more justifications, I gave in. He tried to lighten up the mood by telling me about his crazy friends and how they drank up the whole night and went miles away to pee in front of his friend's ex-girlfriend's house.

Though I was happy about our date going so smooth and peaceful, my inner self was jealous to the core of his girlfriend, Nisha.

Everything was going so perfect until this topic came up and just like pineapples on pizza, it wasn't very pleasing.

He insisted on playing the 'Stare me in the eye' game and whoever would lose will have to fulfil the winner's wish. Which, by the way, could be anything. ANYTHING!

He teased me along the whole game to make sure he wins.

'Don't stare at me like that Kalpana, you'll fall in love.' He nattered.

'You bet.' I played along.

'You will, little princess... Fall in love!' He claimed.

'We'll See.'

Eventually, he won the game. I blinked 5

seconds before the buzzer he had set on his phone. And as per the rules, I had to follow. But Abir played smart, he kept the wish on hold for some other day.

We sat there until dawn. It was a beautiful day minus the Nisha story, how could I like her anyway. Abir insisted on having ice cream before leaving. He treated me with a cornetto and we headed for our respective homes.

***

Abir didn't let me cut the call throughout my way back. We spoke for hours until our phone's battery died. So we decided we would chat after exactly one hour.

After exactly an hour and 10 minutes, the phone buzzed.

'It was a great day! Had fun. Thank you for coming!' Abir texted.

'Did I have a choice?' I replied.

'Haha! You owe me one wish, don't forget.' He replied.

'Roger that sir!'

'I'm sorry for not being there to help you when you slipped. I should have been there for you :(' He texted.

Isn't he the sweetest? I thought to myself hell again!

'It's okay. I can embarrass myself alone :P' I replied.

We chatted for around 20 more minutes before we called off for the day. I remembered the game, staring in his eyes for 90 seconds was like sinking into a deep ocean and going deeper and deeper in it until I dissolve every inch of my soul in it. It was magical.

He was right. I had fallen in love.

Chapter 6 | Popping The Cherry

'Good morning little princess. May I help you?' Abir prompted.

'No Mr... (I looked around to see if there's anyone around us) Busy! I think I can handle this. It's just a leave application.' I assured him.

'Wait, no! Are you planning to leave? You didn't tell me about it!' He exclaimed.

'It's just a month-long leave. I have my exams coming next month, got to study!' I answered.

'Hmm.' He turned away, his nose almost red. He was pissed indeed.

'Abir, I'd be back soon! We're always connected. And we shall be! Don't worry' I said and punched him in his arm.

He turned further away, looking at the window. We were in the HR room and there was no one except the two of us so we had a few moments to spend with each other.

'Smile na… please!' I pleaded with a puppy dog face.

'Okay. But we'd be in touch always. Deal?' He commanded.

'Yes sir!' I accepted.

It had been over a month since we went on our first date. Abir had broken up from Nisha and spent most of his time with me. It was just the office where we would pretend to be strangers. And despite all the efforts, rumours had already started spreading like wildfire about us but we never admitted. It wasn't official either for us to comment on that, so we kept our love-friendship under the wraps.

Suddenly, someone opened the door and entered the cabin. It was the rowdy HR.

'Oh Hi! I was waiting for you.' I said.

'I can see that.' She taunted. Why can't these HRs get a life?

'Well, I am here to submit my leave application. I won't be here for almost a month.' I said, smiling wryly.

Sometimes I would just want to punch her in the face and knock her down. What a B***h she was! And after not approving my appraisal, I had all even better reasons to hate her more.

Nonetheless, Abir and I left the room

silently and continued with our usual office routine.

In the night, at 11:01 PM, he texted, 'Slept?'

'Not yet, was waiting for this guy to text me but guess he's still angry.'

He played along, 'He surely is. But he won't be anymore if the girl can make up for it.'

'So he needs a bribe.' I replied, with a wink.

'Well yes. Anyway, you have my pending wish from our date to fulfil, remember?' He texted back.

'And what would that be?'

'Could be a surprise. You're invited to my place this Sunday. Be there by noon. I'd be waiting.' He demanded.

For a minute, I couldn't react to what he

had just texted. Was he inviting me to his place alone? Is it our special moment? Is he going to propose? I just couldn't hold my excitement.

'Done deal. But tell him I am skipping an important class for him. The surprise better be a good one. Deal?' I snarled.

'As you say, my little princess.'

'Okay then. See you on Sunday.'

'See you!'

And we slept in peace. Life is getting back on track, I whispered to myself. Perhaps this is the beginning of my first real relationship. This is just perfect, I thought to myself with a zillion other thoughts of our soon-to-be relationship before I dozed off.

***

Sunday, 05.04.2015

'Where do you have to go?' asked the bus conductor.

'Munirka.' I responded.

He gave me a ticket and helped me get a seat on the bus. It was my first time after school that I was travelling in a bus. Metro has been my daily commute since then. However, Abir requested to take a bus to reach his place on time.

We spoke throughout the time I was on the bus. He wouldn't disconnect the call for even a second. Our regular days would mostly be the same. He was such a chatterbox. But it all made me feel special. After all, I was the one he wanted to talk to, share his stories, be in touch and be connected to. THROUGHOUT THE DAY, isn't it sweet?

By the time I reached the bus stop at Munirka, it was 11:25 AM, so I was earlier than his asserted time. I called him up and asked him for directions and before he picked up the call, I saw him standing right at the corner of the road, waiting for me.

We went to his house and sat there on the bed-cum-couch. It was a small house, quite like a mini-bachelor pad with one-piece bed and no furniture, a small kitchen and an attached washroom-cum-bathroom. But I didn't care. With Abir, I could be anywhere and be safe.

He had cooked chicken and rice for me. Man, I fell in love with him again! It was such a nice gesture.

'Abir's special dish just for you mam.' He said while serving me the dish.

'Oh Thank you, dear sir. I hope it is not the last dish of my life.' I winked.

'Maybe?' He chirped.

We ate his delicious chicken curry and rice while he told me about his past relationships and his best friend who had just got divorced from her husband. I wondered how relationships can go so bad and despised the idea of breakups or divorce, in this case. But had to accept the truth anyway.

After our lip-smacking lunch, he kept away the dishes and sat right beside me. Slowly, he slipped down to lie and rested at my arm. My heartbeat had already started pumping at top speed.

'You can lie down if you want. You must be tired too.' He insisted.

After pretending to be okay and ignoring the back pain I had earned with the bus ride, I gave in to the idea and laid right next to him.

He held my hand in his and pressed it gently, turned towards me and kept his other arm just below my boobs.

'Your heartbeat is racing little princess.' He whispered in my ears softly.

I lied straight, facing the ceiling and the fan. It was my very first experience of this kind. All the porn videos and erotic tales I had read - nothing of that came to the rescue. So I laid there like a mannequin until….

He pulled me towards him so much that I could feel his chest. Slowly, he moved his arm around my stomach and slipped inside my kurta. I couldn't utter a word. It was a strange feeling.

Pressing his nose against the nape of my neck, he moved his hand further up to caress my melons. He pressed my nipples and played with my boobs. His deep breaths around my neck and the back of my earlobe was arousing me.

He sat to remove his T-shirt and pulled my kurta. Confused and happy as I was, I followed his commands. He removed my kurta and popped open the strap of my bra.

He came over me and we started kissing. His tongue in my mouth made me forget all the worries and confusions in my mind. He kissed my cheeks, my nose, below my lips, above my lips and smooched until we both lost our breath. It was maddening!

He moved his lips down my neck and planted hickies. The tender touch of his lips on my boobs made me go crazy. The relentless pressure of his mouth against my soft nipples was intoxicating. I started moaning.

The air in the room stilled and a hot flash of heat covered our bodies. I could feel his erected organ against my sacred hole. I rhythmically stroked my legs along his. All the chapters around reproduction in biology which we had studied back in class 10th flashed before my eyes. It was magical.

His passionate kisses increased and searching for my bosom, he stroked his hand along my stomach to down there. His gentle presses on my vagina with his long fingers made me moan louder. He held my trousers by the waist and started slipping it down but I resisted. He stopped instantly and nudged his nose on my boobs while he sucked my nipples. He was wild as f**k!

He stood up to remove my pants and my instant reflex action made me stop his hand right there. He looked at me and said, 'Are you stopping me?'

That's it. I could say no no more. He removed my pants and looked down there, then looked at me.

'I wasn't prepared for this.' I nudged and looked away.

My feelings of excitement turned into something strange. I didn't want that to happen too soon. And he was rushing into everything. But I soothed my thoughts with a comforting line - In the name of love!

He dug his forefinger and middle finger deep into my sacred hole, and then pushed another finger in. I moaned loudly. I could see the juice of my cherry on his long fingers. He took his erected organ and planted on the hole ready to dig the traces at all corners inside the cave and started moving in and out.

He groaned quietly while thrusting the inners of my flower. He grabbed me by my boobs and rode on me for about a minute before he plucked out his dick and covered its mouth as I watched the beads of the liquids form at his slit.

And he rushed to the loo, naked.

Before he came back, I dressed up top to bottom, my hands still shivering.

'Uh Oh! Dressed up already?' Abir said, quite surprised.

'Yes, It's already 4:00 PM, I need to leave. No one knows about my whereabouts.'

He nodded, his mind still disapproving the idea of letting me go.

'So… I'll leave now. Bye! See you!' I pushed open the door, waved him bye and exited.

Chapter 7 | The Ultimate Proposal

My leaves had already begun and I avoided Abir's calls for the next three days before we finally spoke after the 'big event'. More than being shy, I was embarrassed. Because A. no one had seen me naked before, and B. no one had seen me naked with lights on. I mean who does that? But Abir had a different level of fetish for having sex with lights on.

On the fourth day, I had to respond.

'Hey, where have you been?' Asked Abir.

'Just home. Was busy with studies and home chores.' I responded.

'And you couldn't spare even a couple of

minutes for me. Hmm.' He exclaimed.

'It's not like that… A… A… Abir, I was just… It shouldn't have happened.' I confessed.

'So you were ignoring me because we got close? Aren't we already are?' He remarked.

'We are… But… I wasn't prepared for it. It was my first. I had wanted my first time to be special.' I said.

'Oh… So it was not special. Fine. I'm sorry, we won't do it again.' He jerked.

'It's not about that Abir. It's just that… I wasn't prepared. You know right, I…' I stopped.

Was I about to confess that I loved him? Oh no! I thought to myself.
'I what? He remarked.

'Nothing, just nothing. You tell me what's happening!' I responded.

'You know right you aren't good with changing topics. So chuck this and tell me that!' He chucked.

'Tell you what? Listen, mom's calling, I have to rush. See you, bye!' I said.

'This is not done.'

'Well! I have to seriously go right now. I'm on call for almost an hour, she would kill me.' I begged.

'Fine. You may leave. But hey! Next time you call me, I wanna hear you say that. Deal?'

'Yeah… okay. We'll see.' I chucked, blushing.

'No, deal or else we don't talk.' He commanded.

'Why are you so stubborn?'

'This is me, you've to accept. I consider the deal done. Bye! Call me soon.'

'Bye.'

Why was he so eager to hear those three magical words from me? Wasn't he supposed to make the first move, as I had seen in all those Bollywood movies? What about my dream proposal? Was I rushing into it too soon?

Honestly, after having sex with him. Like a typical middle-class Indian girl belonging to a conservative family, I had already married him in my mind. Never did I ever believe in the concept of breakups, blame my upbringing for it. Nonetheless, I spent the whole night rehearsing for my first proposal.

'What a perfect love story!' I thought to myself.

***

I had spent the whole afternoon thinking about when to call him. But every time I was about to pick up the phone and dial, my brain would ring its alarm and stop me. These heart-over-mind and mind-over-heart games were only adding on to my anxiousness.

Finally, at exactly 7:15 PM, I went to the roof, locked the door and called him up. There was a tingling feeling running up and down my nerves and butterflies were taking merry-go-rounds in my stomach. Finally, he picked up the phone.

'Hey!' He said, excited.

Chills ran down my spine. I couldn't utter a word.

'Hello? Kalpana, are you there?' He said again, his tone changed.

'Ya… Ya, It's me.' I was nervous.

'So are you ready?' He confirmed.

'Abir, are we really doing this? Can we not…' I pleaded.

'Shut up and say, girl! You remember the deal right?'

'Hmm.'

'So go ahead, I'm all ears!' He exclaimed.

Gathering all my courage and thinking

about all the moments we had till date, I finally confessed my love for him,

'Abir, if roses were kisses, I would have given you a bouquet,
If hugs were trees, I would have given you an environment,
If love was life, I would have given you mine.
So please be mine? I… I… love… you!'

'Didn't hear the last three words, come again?' He teased.

'Abir!!' I said and he giggled.

'Fine, I love you. Happy?' I didn't stutter this time.

'Very well! Great! Good job girl! I'm impressed.' He replied.

'Good job? Isn't it your turn now?' I questioned, my face flushed.

'I will my dear. But I need some time. You know the whole Nisha incident. Give me a few days to clear my head and I'd say it. Okay?' He stated.

'So why did you have to do this today? It wasn't easy for me to confess it too!' I said, pissed already.

'I know. But I wanted to hear it from you first. Let's do one thing, let's meet the coming Sunday, what say? It's been almost a week!' He demanded.

'I'll try.'

'I know you'll come. See you!'

'Bye.'

Holy shit! I had heard that women are complex creatures, but I realised men are no less. He wanted me to propose him just to hear? Did he not feel that way when we had sex? Doubts started blurring my head. What if he says no? What would I do? I could only find out if I meet him this coming Sunday. Mission Abir was on!

Chapter 8 | Sex Therapy

I spent the whole Saturday studying and avoided texting Abir until I received a text from him when the clock struck 11:00 PM.

'Hey! I hope you aren't ditching me tomorrow!' He pinged.

'Well, that might be a possibility. My exams are starting soon, duh!' I replied.

'Don't do this, please! Guess who wants to hang out with you?' He quizzed.

'Have you invited someone else?' I questioned back, confused with his question.

'No dumbo! It's the little Abir! ^_^' He chuckled.

'Little Abir who?' I asked, still as clueless as

before.

'Little Abir!!! Gosh! ;)' He replied.

Someone was getting naughtier day by day! It took me another couple of seconds to realise he was talking about his dick. And as excited I was (courtesy: the hormonal rush), I was equally unsure. He hadn't committed me anything by now. But the lover in me gave in to the temptation…

'Well well! Tell him he has to wait then' I chuckled.

'Don't do this :(' He replied.

We chatted for another hour before we went to sleep. I made sure to not sound excited or break out the news that I am visiting him. It was supposed to be my first surprise! And I couldn't wait to be with him and rest in his arms again!

***

Knock Knock!

'Who is there?' He asked before he reached out to open the door of his house.

'Guess who?' I bubbled.

He opened the door and shouted with glee, 'Oh my God!'

Before I could enter, he had picked me in his arms and hugged me tightly.

'I thought you'd not come.' He softly whispered in my ears.

'That was a surprise!' I chirped.

'I haven't even cooked anything for you yaar!' He exclaimed.

'It's okay! Guess who cooked for you this time?' I beamed.

We smiled at each other and kissed.

He lay me on his not-so-soft bed and in no time, was all over me.

We made out like wild animals. Liplocks, squeaks while smooching, sucking, licking, caressing, everything before he finally dug his organ down in there.

Our foreplay lasted for just a couple of minutes and he directly rushed into the climax. He had bought condoms already, surprisingly! So we had protected sex this time. It was a crazy wild experience.

'I didn't know you had this wild side too, Mr Busy!' I spoke softly while he thrust me with all his might.

'You have to know a lot more then, my little princess.' He responded, still focussing on digging in the cave.

The feeling of his dick penetrating in my vagina was out of the world. His dick, however, was not as big as I had seen in those porn videos. But who sees the size in love, my friends!

A few more seconds and he jerked inside. He pushed his penis the farthest he could in my warm deep hole before he laid flat beside me, he was tired.

He didn't let me wear my clothes this time. And we laid bare in each others' arms for the next few hours.

***

We met three more times before my exams and mostly, it was Sundays. On other days, we would talk over the phone and chat half the day to stay connected. He was one possessive guy, I tell you!

And this also meant, as you may have guessed, that we just had sex on each of our visits. EVERY FUCKING TIME.

Me being a hopeless romantic, I wanted to go out on dates, sit close to each other and enjoy our meals at the cafe, walk hand in hand on the streets of Delhi but No! He just wanted sex. And I could never refuse.

He would do me two, sometimes three times in a single day which left me exhausted. We even tried doing it in his little kitchen. We even tried making out at public places, in public transports and wherever we think there is a possibility. He just wanted me, all of me! And guess who was in love? Me!

In one of the intimate moments in his room, he finally said those three magical words to me - I LOVE YOU which surely was a big turn on for me! And so, we made love again - passion, wild and intense.

Things had finally started settling down.

Chapter 9 | Love is in the Air

My exams were on till the 31st of May, which meant I wouldn't be able to celebrate my birthday yet again. And more than I, Abir was pissed.

'Kalpana, I can't let this happen ya! Can we not meet for even half an hour? He begged.

'That is not possible! I have my exam the next day! Mom won't certainly let me out. You know the situation at home right?' I pleaded.

I didn't realise, this was the first time I actually said no to one of his requests. It felt surprisingly good. Not because I didn't want to meet him, but because I said no! Yes, you read it right - I SAID NO! I had to start learning the trick because his demands had started increasing day by day, which, for some reason, had started to scare me.

'I can't believe you're doing this to me. This is not fair!' he bawled.

'Baby, please understand! We're meeting the day my exams end, I promise!' I replied.

'Fine! Love you! Bye!' He sniffled.

'Love you too!'

Ah! The goodbyes and the good mornings. I still would wake up at least an hour earlier than my routine to call him a 100 times before he would wake up. Even on the days, I felt terribly sick, the days I genuinely wanted to sleep some more and days when I would study the whole night. Love is not easy, my friend!

***

'Happy birthday baby!' He replied.

To my surprise, he had couriered a little soft toy - not a teddy, but a dog. He knew I love dogs, eternally and unconditionally!

'Thank you!

'Did you receive the courier though?' He checked.

'Yes, and it is lovely! My boyfriend knows me well!' I boasted.

'Coz he has the best girlfriend.' He grinned.

Since it was a Monday and he was at work and none of our colleagues knew we were dating, we couldn't talk for more than a few minutes. So I got time to focus on my next day's exam.

At night, he surprised me with his voice note.

He sang a love song for me. And although Anu Malik would have crash-landed on him to stop him singing, I loved the feelings he had put in it and the effort. Girls are so easy to impress sometimes!

Our journey as a couple was going pretty smooth with a few hiccups. And according to the Triangular Theory of Love, our relationship had all the three elements - It had PASSION, it had crazy INTIMACY and it had COMMITMENT. Nonetheless, I was happy and content with my first real experience of having a boyfriend. Unlike those online dates I had on Orkut, I could touch him, feel him, talk to him face to face and go out on dates with him which rarely happened, he made sure we plan our dates at his place only for you know… *winks!

***

Post my last exam, he surprised me by visiting my examination centre, for which he had taken a half-day leave. I introduced him to the only two friends I had made in my college because I would spend most of my Sundays with him and it was the only day we had classes.

We went to Hudson lane to have lunch together. We walked hand in hand on the streets under the scorching heat of the sun, I wasn't dressed at my best, he wasn't best dressed either and his cute gestures only made my day even more special!

'You know you have the most beautiful smile in the world right?' He complimented while having a bite of his favourite Red

Sauce Chicken Pasta.

'*Kuch Bhi!*' I chirped, blushing.

Whenever he would compliment me, this would be my staple answer. '*Kuch Bhi!*' - a way to deny someone's statement sweetly in Hindi.

We ate our meals since it was my treat, so I paid the bill. Not that he paid on our other days, at least. Despite earning almost half his pay and after cutting all possible costs, I would make sure I had enough to feed us both on our outings and shopping. I despised the idea of being totally dependent on a guy but hated wasting money on his useless shopping requests too. After all, I had been brought up in a house where my mom was the real 'man of the house'. She paid for all our expenses right from the very beginning, with no support from her husband or her in-laws. So I never really counted the spends I had made during our relationship including the amount he borrowed me for Nisha's birthday for the very first time, neither he ever said to pay back. We were just two happy souls taking care of each other, the way we could, and most importantly, we loved each other, and that, I felt was enough until I found myself heading towards some real couple problems, problems I didn't know how to deal...

Chapter 10 | Cross Wires

'I am planning to buy a new phone, this one isn't working properly, suggest me some na!' I said to him, while we lay in his rough bed in his little dome.

'I think I know the perfect one for you. What's your budget though?' He replied while playing with my curls.

'I don't know, maybe 10-12k? I can't spend much, you know I have to handle our expenses too.' I snickered.

'Wait, what do you mean?' He stood up, hurting my neck.

'Ouch! What was that Abir!' I demanded, holding my neck.

Without apologizing for the act, he continued, 'You think our expenses are met by you. And I don't do anything?'

'Most of the times. You know it. FYI, you haven't paid for any of the money you asked for. I have forgotten the count already.' I jested.

'So, I don't pay anywhere? I am living on your money. Right!' He wryly smiled.

'Listen Abir, I am not blaming you for anything. You know you don't save anything after sending money to your parents, paying this rent and spending on your *chai-sutta* breaks.' I justified, still claiming the point.

'The last time we went out for lunch, I paid. And have you forgotten about the movie we watched last month together? Oh! I'm sure! How would you remember?' He jested.

'Oh, so we have to count now. Fine. From recharging your metro card to the new curtains in your house and all your Chinese food dates you take me to at Nehru Place, who pays for them? And who spent the whole day running behind you to buy your clothes at *Palika Bazaar?* I pay for your food bills, metro travels, shopping, everything. And you're shouting at me for something we both are aware of?! Wow!' I jerked.

'So it is about the money. I get it now. I thought we're in this together. Guess I was wrong!' He responded, taking a different twist to the quarrel.

'IT IS NOT ABOUT THE MONEY! All I'm saying is I have to manage my expenses according to your comfort. I never say no to you, and that hurts my pockets at times. I have to pay for my graduation too. And you know the situation in my family. Why are we even discussing all this?' I gibed.

But guess who was stuck at the money point? We ended up fighting for 30 long minutes before I put on my clothes, banged the door and left.

We didn't talk to each other for 3 days. Like always, he would expect me to apologize and bow down first. And to save our relationship, I had no other choice. Our relationship was taking drastic turns and it did scare me, a bit too much.

***

'Waiting for you near the metro station, we're going to Nehru Place, come quick!' Abir texted.

'I can't today, I've already told mom I'm on the way home, she'd be really angry!' I replied while walking with Arpita to the same station.

'Fine, I'd stand here until you leave from your metro to your house.' He declared.

I ended up ditching mom for the nth time and went to Nehru Place with him. In these three months, a lot had happened. After last week's fight, I couldn't take a risk to not go with him. Neither was I left with any energy to beg him for a couple of days before he would go back to his normal self. So we went to his favourite Chinese stall.

'So, I'm sure you're liking your new phone, isn't it?' He exclaimed, wanting to hear a yes.

'Yeah! It's nice. But I think Android one would have been better, I'm not used to this new technology.' I suggested while crossing the road to enter the famous Nehru

Place market.

'Oh! You'd be fine. Have no worries when I'm with you.' He bragged.

As we took a turn to go to his the food stall where we had already been a zillion times, he started hinting on his own phone's issues.

'You know, my phone is also not working properly. It heats up soon and hangs too much.' Abir said, looking around.

'Oh!' I responded, preparing myself to eat the same old noodles and chicken platter yet again.

'And the apps also crash too often. I think… I need to buy a new phone too.' He put forth his demand finally.

So now Abir Samant wants a phone also!

Bravo!

'Buy it then! You are a techie, I'm sure you must have already chosen a few options for you.' I responded, not intending to give in to his impractical demand.

'Hmmm.' He responded.

I had been familiar to such responses more than often and had to meet his expected response too, which I duly did, 'Is everything okay?'

'Yes.' He responded and turned to the stall owner to place the order, a big, fat uncle with moustache clinging on his upper lips. He would let go of anything for his 'tache.

I didn't push the conversation further. I was not in the mood for another pointless argument, definitely not in the middle of a public place. We ate in silence.

The next day, Abir didn't call. Neither did I receive any text from him. Although I had seen him using his phone whenever I got a glimpse of him at work, he certainly didn't intend to use his device to talk to his girlfriend.

'All cool?' I texted finally, watching him from a distant shop during our *chai-sutta* break.

He read the message and while he took a drag of his cigarette and didn't respond. I could see the change of expression on his face.

After a few days of acting weird, he finally texted me one fine night, 'Sorry, was unable to call you.'

'Oh! I'm sure there must be some technical

glitches.' I remarked, knowing the excuse he is going to make already.

'A bit! Told you, it isn't working properly.' He responded, continuing his act.

'And I'm sure you must be checking your phone now and then to see if it is working fine or not. Right? -_-' I taunted.

'You're doubting me? You think I am lying?'

'I don't know.'
'So you think coz you got yourself a new phone, I need one too?' He jerked.

'I didn't say anything Abir. But guess who spilt the beans!' I replied.

'You know what! Bye. Enough blaming.' He jerked again.

'I am not going to plead before you to resolve this argument Abir. You are saying things yourself, and expect me to rule out facts which I am not even sure of, this is not happening.' I texted back.

He read, didn't respond.

After 10 minutes of wait, I sent another text before I dozed off, 'Also, if you think you need a phone, you can buy it. I am any-way not asking you to give me anything. Why play a blame game? Just breathe and relax. Good night! Love you!'

No response again!

Is it okay to not give in to such demands from your partner? Is it okay to do anything in love? Is it okay to allow your partner to dominate you even when you know you're not at fault? My mind was full of questions I couldn't answer, puzzles I couldn't solve and self-doubts I only let grew, every f*ck-

VRIDDHI DUA

ing time.

Chapter 11 | Love On The Rocks

'Babe, I love you so, so much! Thanks for the gift!' He texted.

'Wait! You said you're borrowing the money for your phone which you'd return, so how did this become a gift?' I responded, agitated by his indirect hints.

'Hmm. I mean thanks for this… I will return your money. Of course.' He responded, quite shaken by my stance.

'Hopefully this time you will.' I barked.

After 20 days of nagging, I had to buy him the phone he wanted which had cost me a month's salary. I could only see the counter of his expenses increasing and my savings going down the drain. And this had started getting over my head.

The next morning, we had a celebration in our office for the founder's day and we all dressed up for the occasion. I had worn Abir's favourite kurta paired with blue jeans and earrings to match the outfit. Abir was in his usual T-shirt and jeans.

During the party, the HR called out Abir who was chilling with friends and asked a question publically, her objection was obviously to embarrass us both.

'So Abir, I heard you have a thing with Kalpana. Is it true? She asked, everyone's gaze turned towards them.

'Rubbish! Why do you think I would date her?' He interjected.

Arpita pulled me by my arm and whispered to confirm, 'What is this HR saying?'

I shrugged and looked away, stunned by his response. After millions of attempts and all the time we had spent together, Abir had this to express. I never really understood his concept of having a secret relationship.

'But Kalpana's expressions are saying something else,' The HR disputed.

Everyone turned towards me and started staring.

'Too soon to judge! Look at her, she is having a good time with her friends. Why do you even think like that huh!' He gushed.

'Observation my dear.' The HR jerked.

Before Abir could answer, I kept the drink I was holding aside and left the party hall.

After making me wait for over an hour at the metro station, Abir came rushing.

'Hey!' He said as he took the seat next to me.

I didn't respond.

'Why did you leave the party like that? We were supposed to act normal.' He continued.

I looked at him in anger, 'Oh! So I should have waited for some more embarrassment. Right? The whole goddamn office was laughing at me. And I should have stayed! Brilliant' I shrieked, clapping at his immature act.

'It's not like that Kalpana... You know the

HR right, she would have made a scene out of it. So I didn't say anything.' He justified.

'And you think ignoring is the solution? I don't think so.' I concurred.

'I had no choice Kalpana.' He replied, covering my hand with his.

I shrugged his hand and stood up and yelled, 'You're bloody ashamed of calling me your girlfriend and I should be okay with that? What am I? An ATM to you? A sex doll?'

'Stop it Kalpana, don't create a scene out here.' He murmured, clenching his teeth.

'You know what Abir, you need to get your head out of your fucking ass to realize what is happening.' I exasperated and boarded the metro, leaving him sitting right there at the station.

***

After the dramatic incident, returning to office was an uphill task. I didn't want to face anyone, not even myself for the matter of fact. But do slaves have a choice?!

During the working hours, I ignored Abir whenever he would come and try to make a conversation with me. If he would look at me from the corner of his eyes during the lunch break, I would turn and walk away. I was not willing to make up for the blunder he had made.

A few days had passed with no text from him and I wasn't ready to make the first move either. On Saturday night, he drunk called me.

'I..umsoiihjsh' He gibbered.

'Are you okay?' I responded, quite amused by his gibberish tone.

'I… Sorry! I very sorry! I uhsjbnsnm' He blabbered.

'You're not in your senses idiot. We'll talk when you're sober.' I replied.

Before I could complete the sentence, the call got disconnected. I kept the phone aside on the table and took out my diary from the pile of books kept on the corner. My diary had been my support, holding my deepest and darkest secrets. I scuffed through all the entries I had written about our relationship in verses & poems and pulled open a fresh page to pen down my feelings I had been hiding since forever.

'Those eyes speak more than her words,
An ocean of deep emotions,

An expanse of sheer emptiness and died hopes.'

Chapter 12 |Adiós Amor

'Mam, this is for you.' The peon called out, handing me a letter packed in our office envelope.

Everyone in my team turned towards me and insisted on reading the letter aloud to see what's in there, I handed the note to Arpita and asked her to do the honors.

She cleared her throat and read aloud,

'Hey Kalpana!

Don't worry babe, it was a joke. We know you and Abir cannot be a thing. Just look at yourself! Your home-cooked meals and hovering around him won't make him like you. So take a chill pill and cut the drama.

Yours lovingly,
Secret Advisor'

I went red. I had already heard a dozen other comments from fellow teams about how I should 'take a chill pill' and stop running behind Abir and all that crap. But this was way too much. I snatched the letter and ran to Abir's cabin.

I threw the letter at him and bawled, 'What is this?'

Abir read through the lines and looked at me. He was stunned.

'Holy crap! Who's done this?' He asked, flipping the page.

'All thanks to you! And you thought I shouldn't make a deal out of this,' I said and smiled wryly.

'Of course not. How can you be wrong!' I commented.

'Let me find out who did this, It's just a letter. Relax!' He chided.

'Oh ya! Just this letter and dozens of comments from everyone on the floor. I'm sure there must be more coming.' I demurred.

Before he could respond, the HR barged in the cabin and grinned at us, 'Is everything okay you guys?'

'Ya! It's just people have been after her since the party ended. But we're sorting it out, don't worry' He chucked.

The HR stared at us and walked out of the cabin.

'Okay listen Kalpana! We'll handle this, but

if anyone catches us together like this, we both will be in trouble! I'll take care of this I promise, and I will see you in the cabin in tea time today too. But can you for now...'

'You know what? Just suck it up.' I said and left his cabin, banging the door behind.

***

35 missed calls and 43 messages later

'Where the hell are you?' Abir shrilled on the call.

'As if you care?' I shrugged.

'I had been trying to connect with you since so long. What's wrong with you!' He chided.

'Just trying to correct the wrong doings of the past' I responded.

'I called to tell you that Priyanka, that skinny girl from Team A had sent that letter to you. I've spoken to her, she's ready to apologize to you for the act.' He answered.

'Hmm.' I replied.

'Don't be like me Kalpana, I won't be able to handle this. Please!'

'I have no answer Abir. You can't even realize how bad it feels when the whole office mocks at you. I hope you're happy, you saved your so-called image!'

I continued, 'You know, I had really thought this was my forever, we are forever. But... anyway, mom's calling, I'll talk to you later.'

'You're overthinking honey! You'd be just fine. I love you!' He prompted.

'Hmm,' I responded and disconnected the call.

That night, I cried my heart out. I felt shattered and broken. My whole world revolved around someone who didn't care a darn about me or us. I grieved in silence and opened by diary to penned down a note,

'She had love in her eyes,
And pain in her heart.
She couldn't receive the love,
And never released the pain.'

***

After spending the weekend in isolation and the conversation we had on ending things back in the office cabin, I was already prepared for the 'The End' of our love affair.

Swans mate for life, but we were humans! We just took a little longer to realize that we were perfect misfits for each other! And although we had mutually ended things up, I had to have a proper closure to it.

So I called Abir to his favourite spot, Nehru Place after office.

To my surprise, he was before time to see me at the station. Usually, he would come 15-20 minutes late. But this day was different. We didn't talk much until we reached the market and went to eat at the food court.

'You seem quite quiet' He noticed.

'No. I'm fine!' I said, the classic reply of a woman when she is not.

'So, what would you have?' He asked.

'Anything, you can choose and order for both of us.' I said and started fidgeting my fingers.

He went and got us a chicken bucket, the second surprise of the day - he got my favourite food to the table!

We ate in silence until I spoke, 'Abir, I need to discuss something.'

He looked at me and said, 'Go ahead! I had been waiting for you to speak up!'

'I mean, there isn't much to say about this. But, I mean, I hope we're on the same page for ending this arrangement we had between us.' I stated.

'You're rushing into conclusions Kalpana! We really don't need to do this' He exclaimed.

'Probably, but I don't think I have the courage to do this few months or years down the line. We fight more than often, awkwardness has creeped in between us and… and the void between is only getting deeper.' I restated.

I took a deep breath and continued, 'I can't do this to me, not anymore ya! It's just… too much'

'Hmm. So this is your final decision. We're not a thing anymore, right?' He countered.

'Yes.'

'Fine then. You anyway needed a reason to leave, so be it.' He shrugged.

I looked at him and smiled, 'You and your dialogues uh! See, I have done my best I could to keep this relationship going, but everything has a limit, I seem to have crossed mine long ago.'

'Was it even love?' He quipped.

'I don't know. Maybe it was, or maybe it was not. Love is a beautiful feeling Abir! And we create our own definition of love in our lives. But it gotta be mutual to work it out. Our definitions mismatch, we mismatch!' I retorted.

'I'm sorry... I know it's way too late to say it but I genuinely am. I... I messed up everything.' He concurred.

'It was my fault too. I never loved or valued myself. And your jokes only added on to my self-doubts. But I think it's time to take the steering wheel in my hand, if this wouldn't have happened, I would've never known. So thanks for that!' I conceded.

He gazed at the table and pursed his lips.

I smiled at him and spoke, 'Goodbye! Hope you find your definition of love soon!'

He glanced at me for a few seconds and finally said, 'Goodbye... little princess!'

We hugged each other one last time and left.

Epilogue

Three and a half years later

'Are you ready mam?' Mr Nair said.

'Absolutely! Let's hit it!' I said.

In a few minutes, the anchor announced on stage,

'Let's call upon our most awaited guest and the author of this book. So please put your hands together for Miss Kalpana Koushik!'

I walked up to the stage and took my place next to the anchor. The view of the audience cheering was absofuckinglutelyawesome!!

'Thank you, guys! Let's hear from our author about her debut book!' The anchor affirmed.

'First of all, I would like to thank you all to come here and be a part of my first book launch! A few years ago, I was just a teenage girl losing her identity and living on the opinions of others. And I think that's a common problem among us. We do things we don't want, pretend to be someone we don't like and look at ourselves in the mirror to only find flaws. But you know what's worse? It's us trying to please people we don't know and forget our own individual identity. So here I am, a common girl with an uncommon dream, fighting the odds to become the best version of myself. Because better is temporary, best endures! And now if someone asks me what's up? I proudly say, my self-esteem.'

Cheers galored.

About the Author

An avid reader and a dance enthusiast, Vridhi Dua has established her name in the field of content and marketing at a young age. Born on May 20, 1996, she has been born and brought up in the capital city of India, Delhi.

Her life story had been published among selected few on Puma's website for their #DoYou movement while she was still in college. She has done her graduation in

B.A. English Honours from Delhi University and has published her write-ups to over 1000 websites to date. Having her roots in a Punjabi Family, she loves her food and enjoys experimenting with new things. According to her, writing happened to her while she was working for an NGO and has been hooked to her pen since then. Her love for reading extends from Durjoy Dutta to Paulo Coelho.

Connect with her:

Instagram: *@thatcurioussoul*

Facebook: *@https://www.facebook.com/thatcurioussoul/*

Twitter: *@https://twitter.com/vriddhidua*

Or write to her at:

Gmail: *vriddhi.dua@gmail.com*

Once upon a time in Delhi, there was a girl named **Kalpana Koushik**. Her whole life takes a turn after her mom is diagnosed with a deadly disease and she lands up in a job right after school. There, she falls for a guy called **Abir Samant**. Things take a scary turn after they get into a secret relationship.

Will they last forever? Or will they have a fatal end? Discover what the two unfold for themselves!

Vriddhi Dua is an accomplished writer holding her position in the field of Content and Marketing for over 6 years. Dance enthusiast and a traveller by heart, she is inclined towards entrepreneurship and has been setting benchmarks at a young age.

UPTOWN OGRE

USA TODAY BESTSELLING AUTHOR

AVA ROSS